The Last Page

RICHARD FIERCE

Contents

Introduction

It burns.

If nothing else, it burns. In the dark—in the dark, I cannot see it. But I can still *feel* it. Even after all these years, the memory of it remains; burned upon the stygian depths of my expanded being like a brand upon my chest. To be marked by one's deeds—if my deeds were to be judged by the mark that I carry—I would deserve the fate that has befallen me.

My fate? An ongoing divine Comedy of Manners—a dialogue of dry wit, intrigue, and cleverness long since gone trite with its latest telling. I sit upon a great throne in a chamber that is all my own—a part of a vast empire whose reputation of fear will endure the ages, if not the power behind it all. My domain spans the distance with pure, unadulterated power, and cold, immoral expansionism.

This was a story begun with violent ambition—an ambition that consumes all in its path. It was—it *is*—an ambition that burns. But like all flames, it shines brightly, spreads across barriers, destroys them, and reduces all into ashes. When born, fire consumes its womb to ashes, but eventually to those ashes must it return. Then there is darkness—the cool, soothing blackness that cocoons me, protects me, and suffocates me.

It is the source of my strength, you see. To call down darkness upon my enemies, and to blot out the very light that I once loved, and now hate so much. Although, now that I ponder over this conundrum, I see that distinctions between hatred and love, darkness and light, tend to blur together in my mind and cancel each other out. Was I blinded by the blazing light or arrogance, or made sightless by the darkness that is my power?

Whatever the casualty of my existence, I still have one mote of humor left, even after all this time. Namely, I still possess my sense of irony. What is it, you ask? I will tell you—that I, a Lord of Darkness—am as blind as the drones under my command. Only in my element can I see the black blood of this pen purging me of my painful years of brooding, staining the purity of the parchment that will spread, surgically divide, and consume the white. A fitting analogy considering that I finish the last page of the story in that fashion. A story ends in darkness. Of course, it can begin from darkness as well...

1

Ol-arys khyl' altai

The Book is oneself infinite, Word stronger than sword, the Pen possibility incarnate.

A STORY DOES BEGIN with but a single word. Words are powerful things, although for the most part, they are indeed taken for granted. Most simply use them to communicate with as minimal difficulty as they can—appreciating only their most pragmatic and utilitarian of uses. However, there are very few who can understand that words are the outlet of one's innermost ideals—an expression of an idea, or its form, while the meaning or idea behind it is its essence.

When used properly, they can be great and persuasive enough to create and preserve governments, philosophies, and religious movements. But then there are a select few individuals in all the Realms who have an inherent understanding, that there are some *words* whose essence makes up a greater whole than anyone could have imagined—representing grand and ancient cosmic powers undreamed of.

So yes, words are important. But over time, a word or even its cosmic equivalent can lose its meaning. Governments grow corrupt, faulty, and weak. Philosophies are used so many times that their essences become lost in the sophisms that become their forms. Religious institutions, once founded on open spiritualism, become hollow, and intolerant. It was from the latter that I came—trapped and blinded within the clutches of the fanatical, religious zeal that was my birthright. So maybe I was wrong. Perhaps my story did begin in light——a searing and unforgiving one.

I do not remember the exact name of the Realm I was born in, but I remember what it was like. The buildings of my city were enormous and oval-shaped, made from a stone of the purest white, and their windows were crystalline and multifaceted. Everyone called it the City of Light. It was beautiful and pristine, I will grant you. At night, the city glowed with a radiance that would have fooled many foreigners into thinking that it was in eternal morning.

Yet the Great Temple of Oru dwarfed even the purity of the Realm's capital city. It was a monolith of an alabaster cathedral with a multitude of glimmering rainbow lights refracted from the Crystal Spire which lay in its center—an ornate dagger embedded within a sinner's soul. It also served as the heart of the Theocracy of Oru.

And when I had my migraines, I remember having to hide in the darkest, deepest chamber I could find in order to keep away from that infernal, incessant light that everyone else loved so much. Otherwise, the glow of the buildings and walls would blind me, and the shining light caught in the diamond edges of the windows would pierce my skull like thousands of tiny, white-hot shards of pain. The very sight of the Great Temple to the Realm's patron deity itself would have probably induced a seizure in me in those days. So I hid from that light.

Perhaps that was only a small part of the reason my father despised me so much—a small, yet essential part.

My family were devout worshipers of Oru, much like everyone else in most, if not all, of the Realm. However, let me explain that when

I say *devout*, I am really attempting to create an understatement. Perhaps the words *obsessive*, *fanatical*, and *small-minded* would better suffice.

Oh yes, and the only difference between my family and other citizens of the City of Light was that we were more *devout* than even they. Or at least it seemed that way when you were a member of the family containing a Priest of Oru. My father was the patriarch of our family in every sense of the word—ruling over our minds, bodies, and souls as he did with the rest of the populace. My mother, although she was subservient to his whims, was just as pious—if not gentler. She had to deal with the whims of my two other siblings—a bunch of miserable, whining brats.

I remember my mother most of all. She was tall, and willowy, her long hair was brown—almost black. Those born with black hair in the City of Light were usually shunned as creatures of darkness, and killed when they are born. My mother, however, belonged to a noble family and she was saved from this tradition by being put into an arranged marriage with my father—a man almost twice her age.

Sometimes I wonder whether or not she wished for the death they denied her. There were times I thought I saw roots of black in her coiled, brown hair.

Her life was not that much more merciful. My Priest father ignored her for the most part, letting her three children drain the life and vitality out of her, like the little blood-sucking leaches we were at that age. While I grew out of infancy all too quickly, the other leaches grew up to be full-fledged vampires—little monsters that grew stronger off her growing weakness. There were times I would look at the deep lines engraved onto her visage and see some semblance of the beauty she must have possessed at one time.

I must have been my mother's favorite, even though she never spoke about it. Then again, she never spoke much of anything. Long ago, something must have happened to her throat. I knew this because I saw a fine slash scar on her throat where her voice box was located. Indeed, as with many organized patriarchal cultures modeled for a *male god* by *pious* men, one general rule is that a woman should be seen and not heard. Another tradition in our Realm was that if a woman speaks out against her patriarch, or shows any evidence of learning something she should not know, he has the right to rob her of her voice.

Perhaps he did that to her, but whether it was successful or not was a mystery. Indeed, there were many whisperings about such things among the servants when they thought that I was ignorant or unhearing. Of course, such talk was rare because they wanted to keep their voice boxes intact. But when I looked into my mother's eyes, I saw a keen intelligence behind her submissive facade. In case you are wondering, despite the fact that she did not talk, I knew her to be a pious woman because I always saw her silently praying, and bowing before our altar at home. Most likely that was all she had ever known. She needed someone to pray to when my father became angry with her—to pray to for mercy, and to pray to for forgiveness to have made the first prayer. If her voice was undamaged, she learned to hide it very well. Able to speak or not, she protected me from the worst of my father's wrath.

In the eyes of the citizenry, my father was a divine figure—a living incarnation of Oru's power in the mortal plane. In his robe of purest white and woven gold symbols, he recited his sermons, his blessings, and occasionally curses, for the masses. They believed him and the other Priests to be deified saints made flesh once more—wise beings that needed to be venerated without question.

In reality, my father was a solid, stout man with thinning iron-gray hair, and a perpetually dead-set expression on a pockmarked face. The robes and the headdress made him look like some divine saint, but underneath the pristine facade he wore in public, I knew him to be an intolerant, black-hearted, and petty tyrant. In other words, the proverbial wolf in sheep's clothing. I will not go into the kinds of actions he committed, in his so-called *divine* role, nor will I waste anymore paper and ink to record down his mad rambling. The only ranting that you will see here is mine—for at least mine has a method, and a reason of origin behind it.

At any rate, it was custom (as were many other things) for the eldest born of a Priest to follow in his sire's footsteps in the worship of the Almighty Oru, and my father had high expectations for me. Or at least he called them high. I called them impossible. My other siblings were left alone and nothing was expected from them, but since they were the children of a powerful Theocrat certain allowances were made for them. In other words, they did whatever they wanted to whomever or whatever they wanted. But such was not my case.

I was, at best, a frail child. When I think about it, my father had considered killing me when I was but an infant. His rationale was that he wanted a strong, healthy heir, not a weak, pathetic, little wretch like me. Somehow, perhaps because of my mother's good graces, I was spared—allowed to live a life of indoctrination, abuse, and neglect when I was not needed. Obviously, I was never really that talkative.

Early in my life, I learned that talking back to my father brought consequences. His physical abuse became less constant as I got older, and it began to transmute more into mental and verbal lashings. Every day I learned his prayers, the ceremonies, and the rituals.

In the classroom at the Great Temple, my education continued along with those of the other children.

"And so Oru came to our people aeons ago to end the blasphemies that kept our Realm a warring, heathen backwater. We learned of how He had no physical form, and that He had told our people to gather the wisest and eldest of men together so that He might bestow His divine knowledge upon them," I remember our teacher explaining with a stern face. "Can anyone tell me what the role of the female is in the Realm of Oru?"

A girl raised her hand. "Women cannot learn how to read or write because we shed blood monthly. Blood begets blood. To teach Those Who Shed Blood," she recited one of the laws of Sacred Text dictated to her by word of mouth, "would be to allow the bloodshed and division to rise anew. Only can a true Handmaiden, ordained by Oru, be considered pure, and even she is not taught how to read or write," she ended off, and our teacher nodded approvingly.

The female students, who were usually Handmaidens-to-be—*divine concubines* in the making—were taught orally. Only males could have this knowledge and enforce the Will of the Light—for they were closer to Him, made in His image, and did not go through menstruation. We males were taught through reading and writing. But even we had our limitations.

I also learned that those first High Priests and their lesser brethren had been oath-bound to reproduce with the purified Handmaidens of their Lord and teach their oldest male heirs the wisdom of Oru—to read and write only of His greatness and nothing more. I learned and recited these things under my father's stern, cold, dark eyes, and his equally cold iron fist.

And every day I felt my soul waning. It was as though a fist closed over it—suffocating the life out of it. Perhaps that was my first taste of darkness—the suffocation and the inflicted blindness. Yet I did have one mode of escape—a mode that even he could not control.

My writing.

I wrote of imaginary places, strange creatures, and people much different from our own. There was no mention of Oru or the Theocracy in those writings that I held dear. It was an outlet for my imagination, and my imagination alone. I could build worlds for myself—worlds born from infinite possibility. Each of these stories or writings also helped ease my headaches—pains in my skull that would grip me when I hadn't written anything in a long time. No one knew about my little

transgression against one of Oru's command-
ments.

As I became an adolescent, I ventured outside more often and explored the rest of the
city—particularly its marketplaces. I bought
books from the other Realms—material that
was legally censured by the Theocracy under the strictest of penalties. After I read the
books, I generally sold them back to some
traders, furtively glancing around to make
sure that no one recognized me and that I was
not being followed.

One day, another person—a girl—sought
some books from a trader that I also desired.
We bartered over those books, and she was
furious at me for getting in her way. "I want
these books," she hissed at me, the fire behind
her eyes all too evident. "Some of us need to
read so that we can survive another day."

"For this book? Oh spare me, please. It is a
bloody storybook."

"Some of us," her voice was still fierce, but there was an odd catch in her throat. "Some of us need all the fantasy we can get our hands on..."

I closely examined her face. That was perhaps the only important thing that my father did tell me, was that if you stared hard enough into a person's face, or their eyes, you could divine their intentions, or at least get an idea of what they were feeling. It helped him when he had to go manipulate the masses.

The girl was smaller than me; almost petite. I cannot describe her body's appearance even now. If you were to compare her to a structure, an architect would say that she possessed very few angles, and was mostly composed of curves.

Indeed, her arms, legs, and hips were shaped and connected in smooth, fluid curves. Her skin was smooth, slightly darker than mine, and her pearl-white teeth bit into her ruby lower lip. Her reddish-copper hair was shaped into curls, and a strand of it hung over her left eye. When I looked into her large, brown eyes I was transfixed by the feral nature behind them, the raw need for something more, and the voraciousness for learning.

I knew that one look from those eyes would allow me to commit the ultimate blasphemy. She was both a Blooded One—not blessed by the Theocracy to be a Handmaiden—and she looked like she had exotic, foreign origins. She wasn't even part of our religion.

"How much do you know how to read?" I asked her.

"Huh?" she looked surprised; her gaze suggested otherwise.

"Well?"

"Um, a little, I guess. Why?"

"I can help you," I offered.

Her eyes seemed to devour my own, and I thought for a second that her face softened.

"It's been a while since someone has come to talk to me. Who are you? You don't seem to be from around here."

I gave her my name. And she gave me hers.

"I—I will see you again. Here," I gave her the book and paid the trader.

"You didn't have to—thank you," and she ran off.

Victorie was her name.

2

Outside the knowledge of my parents, I spent much of my time with Victorie. The reason I got away with it for the most part was that my father had duties at the Great Temple.

All this time, we avoided anyone who would notice us together. Because my father had the habit of putting the fear of Oru into the populace, all people tended to notice me, and wanted to gain favor with my father—even if it meant telling him about Victorie.

Eventually, Victorie had gotten used to my continued presence, and I got to know more about her personal convictions. In some ways, it was as though I had befriended a wild animal by giving it space and slowly moving around it.

At one point, she asked me what it was like to be the son of a high-ranking Priest of Oru. I did more than tell her. I managed to smuggle my schoolbooks out of my house, and I tried to explain to her how the whole system worked.

"That is no life," she flatly stated to me. "Basically, you do what you're told, and if you don't agree, you get punished by being ex-com—what does that bloody word mean?"

"Excommunicated," I specified for her. "It means that you are banished from the religion you once belonged to, and you no longer have its benefits."

"What _benefits_? Wouldn't you want to get out of that hell-hole?!" she exclaimed. I didn't meet her eyes. Then we spent an hour going over another chapter. "What is this about Blooded Ones?"

"They are talking about females. Oru made men in his image and women as the means to continue them. The reason they are called Blooded Ones is because they go through, um, cycles of menstruation."

"Thank you, I know what it is," she smoothly answered. "But why are we the inferior ones?"

"I don't know. Because they," notice how I did not say I, "believe that to give women power is to allow blood to spill again."

The defiance behind her voice said more than even her words. "That is such garbage. Garbage! And then—look at this. In order for a woman to be allowed to associate with a Son of Oru, she must go through a cycle of purification. She must do so in order to fulfill her ultimate and only purpose—to bear male heirs to continue the Blessed Race?" she ended with incredulity.

I realized then that there were some things I could not justify. The force that drove me to know I lacked the power to explain the actions of my own culture.

"Well, I will never let a man control me. Ever." She regarded me for a long while, assessing my eyes as I did hers when I first met her. "You don't believe in this either, do you?"

It was that very realization that brought me further away from my theological imprisonment and closer to understanding her. Victorie wanted to tell me about her views on existence. Instead of telling me, though, I encouraged her to write these ideas down. As time progressed, her rudimentary writing skills became stronger, and she started writing small poems and short polemics.

When her main work was done, she handed it to me. "I don't know if I did this properly, but can you look over it?"

Once I agreed, I took the papers from her. It read: *It is said that Oru created Nature and then He made us. But if He made men to be superior, and if He were All-Knowing, then why did He give women or the 'Blooded Ones' the potential to do the same if it is forbidden? Why give us these desires and deny us the satisfaction? Why forbid any of us to indulge in happiness?*

I read on. *I believe that Nature made us first, and that some among us created Oru to enslave the rest of us, to rob us of our simple delights, and to enforce unnaturalness upon us. I still believe that we have freedom, if not paradise—the freedom to survive and the freedom to die. I want to be free*, her material confided. *We were born from Nature, and we will go back to it when we die. I want to go back while I still live.* Her words created an odd pang inside of me. *What do you want?*

"To be free like you," I softly whispered to myself.

She also told me about her family. "We were exiled from our Realm of Arema when some raiders came and destroyed our home. It was a beautiful place, our Realm—a place of vast and ancient trees. You could sense the life flowing there. Not like this Realm—filled with cities, and rigid boundaries."

So she and her parents moved to this Realm, where the Theocracy would not accept them due to their *outsider heathen* origins, and it left them in the poorer and more squalid districts of the City of Light. In the end, her parents couldn't support her, and they abandoned her to fend for herself. She had to steal for sustenance in order to survive. The word sustenance had a broad definition in her mind. Not only was it nourishment for her body, but for her mind as well.

As time went on, we became close as I confided my secrets to her about my life, about how I was dissatisfied with the existence my father wanted for me, and how I got sick sometimes with migraines that seemed to get worse as I got older.

Once, I cried convulsively in her arms when the pain inside me was too intense to bear, suffocating me, choking me. "I'm so sick of this," I sobbed. She would merely sit there and rock me gently, whispering, "It's all right. Shush. It's all right..."

It escapes me when Victorie realized that I was more than just a friend. Perhaps it had been one of the many stories I read to her. I cannot recall.

"I loved that story," she breathed, after I had read it out to her. "I felt like I could almost touch the worlds and beings you wrote about." Just as I was going to look away from her bashfully, she kissed me. Then I returned the gesture, until we both expressed the passion that had been hiding just above the surface of our relationship.

Our first kiss had been sweet and innocent. How could anyone have had the sheer gall to say that what we had was wrong or unholy?

It wasn't fair. No, you don't understand. I was a man, and she was a woman. Or if we were too young to be given those roles, I suppose you could say I was a young boy, and she, a girl. Better yet, let us just say that we were male and female—two genders whose relations with each other were supposed to be natural. So how could it have been wrong? Of course, every contradiction has its scapegoat, does it not? This one's excuse had been religion. For, after all, did not the spirit transcend the flesh?

Oru ruled the All in wisdom and compassion. But if He created the All—would He have not also created the simple joys between men and women? Would He not have accepted all beings that He created as His children? But why then did His Priests—His thrice-damned Priests—condemn our association? If the spirit really did transcend the flesh like the Priests had preached, then did it actually matter where the souls came from?

"I love you," she said one day when our young blood ran hot, and we lay expended in each other's arms.

From that moment onward, I stopped praying to that god—that unseen, removed, inhuman god of a Light that hurt my eyes and invaded my privacy. I always felt guilty—guilty for existing, for displeasing my parents, and for the writing of things that did not exist by Oru's creed and only for my own selfishness. Most of all, I felt guilty for having Victorie love me—loving me and being unable to return the favor. But no more. Ever since I was born, I accepted my abuse in silence and without question, until I realized that the philosophy I was forced to serve would rob me of the woman I loved.

They said that it was profane for a son of Oru to touch a heathen Bleeding One. They said that Victorie was a Bleeding One. I loved her for that, too. I wanted her to bleed all over me, all over my soul—to allow her fierceness of spirit, her simple, raw passion for life to eat away the dead, sterile whiteness of my spirit and invigorate both my body and my mind. I wanted to live. To live without fear, or resentment.

She would become my Victorie—against all the years of suppression and isolation—against the guilt as unnatural and artificial as the sterilized pristine womb that nurtured it. In her dark brown eyes, I lost myself to the natural beauty within her. Then, one day, things changed.

Somewhere along the line, I found out that Victorie had known how to read and write all along. The reason I knew was that she told me that another had taught her before I did. She told her friend all about me, and apparently her friend wanted to see me as well. At first, I was unsure, but I knew Victorie would never betray me.

"She tells me she knows how to cure your headaches," she explained to me.

That notion did intrigue me. They were very painful indeed. My fingers would spasm when they came to me, and writing only re-lieved them for a time. When we found Vic-torie's friend, she was hiding in the shadows of an alleyway. Once I saw her, I marveled at the contrast between Victorie and the woman I saw before me.

She was pale-skinned—her flesh alabaster as the walls of the Holy City itself. The woman had long and luxurious strands of black hair that served as a halo framing her faintly cherubic, fragile visage. Her face was impassive, but there was life behind her dark gray eyes—a gaze that seemed to devour the details of everything directly in its sight.

"So," her voice had a lilting tone to it, almost making it musical, "he is your friend, Victorie?"

"Yes, Master," and I saw my beloved slightly bow toward her.

"Pardon me," I questioned the woman, "But might I inquire as to who you might be?" I learned my etiquette ages ago after my father beat it into me several times.

"Hmm, polite too, I see. Quite the way with words," she gave me a smile. "There is no need for such formalities. We are all friends here—you to Victorie, and myself to her as well. But you do seem curious about my ti-tle, dear boy," her smile quirked. "Not many women here have such titles, do they?"

"As far as I know, only that of Handmaid-en," I admitted.

"Ah, yes. Well, obviously I am not from around here. Neither is Victorie. In the Realm I come from, my title is given to those who have students. My name, at the moment, is not mine to give. Perhaps some other day I will tell you. However, you may call me Master if..." her voice fluidly trailed off as she reached over and touched my brow. "You say you have headaches, young sir?"

I tried to answer, but a faint whispering sound in my ears had momentarily distracted me. It might have just been my imagination, but the woman traced some kind of shape on my forehead.

"Do not worry, my dear," she gently said. "I believe that your headaches will ease somewhat. Yes, Victorie here did not exaggerate. You are just the person I have been looking for. Do come in, I have something to show you if you are interested," she pointed at a doorway that I had not noticed before, and went inside.

"C'mon," Victorie pulled me closer to her, her eyes radiant. "You know those worlds you tell me about all the time? She can help you find them, or even make them," the tone of her voice was urgent. "I know I lied to you before, but I couldn't let anyone know about her. I had to trust you. Now I do. Do you trust me?"

I had to. There was something about the woman that intrigued me. We followed her through the doorway I hadn't seen earlier and found ourselves in a dimly lit chamber composed of simple wooden floorboards, with a desk, a sleeping pallet, and a fireplace.

"'Come into my parlor, said the spider to the fly'," laughed the woman, gesturing at some chairs near her own. "Just a little literary humor among equals. Please sit down. Do not worry, my dear boy. Neither your Priest father nor his cronies will find you in here."

"How did you know?" I asked in what might have been a combination of shock and horror.

"I have my sources. Besides, would not one have heard mention of one of the rulers of the Theocracy?" she replied. "I sent Victorie to find you."

"Who are you?" I repeated.

"You could say that I am a missionary from another Order, sent here to find those who have the potential to be something greater than what they already are. I already found Victorie. Now it seems I am fortunate to have found another."

"It's true," Victorie told me. "I didn't completely lie to you. I had trouble with this Realm's language, and you did help me with that. My parents did have to abandon me so that they could survive," her eyes flared briefly with old pain. "But they knew that I would have certainly died if I stayed with them. I live with my Master. She has shown me such wonderful things, beautiful things..."

"She now lives with me, as I teach her," said the woman. "Sometimes I send her out to scout for others like you. I see that you are still unaware of what to think of me. Fair enough. Perhaps Victorie can better illustrate my position than I can. Victorie, show him what you can do." Victorie's Master pushed some paper across the desk.

Victorie folded back the sleeve of her dress, and I saw that there was something attached to her wrist—a small pouch of some kind. She bent her hand back, palm first, and used the other to extract a writing utensil from the pouch. I had never known her to posses such a thing. The pen she had was made of a rich brown, grainy substance, with a sprout of something green on its top. It was almost like a twig, or some piece of a tree that was molded and shaped into a pen. Somehow, it seemed appropriate for Victorie. She always seemed more akin to something feral and wild than what many people deemed *civilized*.

Victorie began to write on the parchment. It was a script I had never seen before—a series of symbols in forest-emerald ink. The words, if that was what they were, were as curved as Victorie's body. When I saw the symbols, something inside me stirred, stronger than even the greatest physical lust I had ever experienced. She leaned forward, her copper curls falling over her one eye. Her face was intent, her brown eyes alight with a joy I had neither seen nor experienced before—even when we lay in each other's arms.

What happened next took me completely off-guard. The surface of the brown desk became fluid, and a large bump rose from it. It grew arms—many, many arms, and foliage of green, red, orange, and violet began to sprout from its upraised limbs. As Victorie kept writing, I saw a small tree form itself. But as I looked closer, I saw a face appear on it—a visage similar to Victorie's own smiling at me. Victorie stopped writing, and the thing became liquid and shapeless again, retreating back into the surface of the wood from whence it came.

I wasn't scared, or even shocked. Instead of running, I asked, "How—how did you do that?"

She put her pen back into her wrist-pouch, a small, mischievous smile on her face. "What I did was I wrote of the living energy that was once in the wood before it became a desk. Then, I—expanded on it—and it began to live again. Then I allowed it to grow for a while, and added a few, new characteristics."

"Now, Victorie," her Master chided, "that hardly even begins to explain what had happened. I shall have to do my best to explain. My Order is called the Scrybal Guild. We represent a small few among the Realms that understand the difference between writing," and she took out her pen and scribbled something down, "And this word—wryting."

"What?" I breathed. "But how did you do this?"

In the near beginning of my tale, I'm afraid I didn't do justice to my definition of wryting. Perhaps the person who was to be my Master could have outlined it best when she first introduced it to me.

"There are writers, and then there are wryters," she explained. "We belong to the latter category. The difference is that while a writer can have a grasp of the form of a word, and perhaps some basic essence, wryters understand and can grasp both the form and the essence of the Words that make our reality what it is. With it, we can manipulate certain aspects of Creation itself. And you can do so as well. You have the Gift."

"It's true," said Victorie. "You are a much better wryter than even I. There is so much my Master can teach you. When you taught me the basics of this Realm's language, it helped me create more descriptive sentences. You have a gift for words in that language. But once you learn Runic, there will be no boundaries for you. None at all."

"Runic?"

"Yes," said her Master. "Do you want to know? Do you want the skill? I can make it happen. Think of it, my dear. Endless worlds at your beck and call, and the limitlessness of imagination made incarnate. There will be risk in this, but the rewards far outweigh them. I know what you want—that you love to write. So tell me what you want to say."

I remembered all the days I sat in my home, the endless days of indoctrination, of abuse, of being enslaved, of watching others be enslaved; of writing and never being satisfied because I knew that I could do better. I wanted to see my visions come alive, to make me happy, to make me feel more wonder than even Victorie's wryting. I wanted my soul to soar in the ultimate glory of Creation unfettered.

"Yes," I replied. "Master..."

3

WHAT I LEARNED WITH my Master and Victorie made me feel more alive than I had ever been. Under my new Master's protection, I learned the written language of Runic—realizing that each symbol represented a summarization of detailed descriptions. To their delight, I progressed very quickly and began mastering Words that even Victorie—who had been a pupil of this Art long before me—didn't even know.

The people who used these words were my people, my Master told me. They had various names throughout the Realms, but they had adopted one name, one Word that suited them quite well. A person of the Word, a wryter of one's own creations, and co-wryter of the Greater Story of the Prime Wryter Itself. They—we—are called Scrybes.

With Pen in one hand, and Book in the other, we crossed Realms of diversity and made almost whatever we desired with the written language of Runic—the ancient language of Creation itself. We understood one saying, the core belief of Scrybalism: *Ol-arys khyl' altai*.

There were six stages to a Scrybe's development: Student, Novice, Apprentice, Disciple, Master, and Grandmaster. Students and Novices were taught in classes—as were Victorie and I in a rudimentary kind of way. I had already achieved the equivalent of Apprentice, although my schooling was informal, and I didn't know what sect I wanted to be in. A Disciple had basic Scribal skills and belonged to a sect. They were usually called Scrybes. The

Masters were Scrybes that taught others, and Grandmasters; they had more or less mastered the Art itself.

Our Master told us of the Guild and its home-Realm in Scryuune. When I asked what it looked like, she said she couldn't tell me because it defied all descriptions. All she said was, "It is a place where literacy is embraced above all else—where Words are not merely on paper."

I learned that the Guild was divided into seven sects. There were the Scroll-wrytes who made short-term Words on scrolls or parchments that anyone—including non-wry-ters—could use. The Rune-forgers inscribed Words of Power onto surfaces like metal or wood to either augment their strength or re-form them. She said that it was rumored they even made automatons—mechanisms of inanimate material that could move or even think. The Warscrybes were a warrior-caste that used strategic wryting in battle as their swords, and the Veil-weavers were those who could see into people's dreams, and could shape them as well. I might have belonged to the latter if things had turned out differently.

Then there were Chronoscrybes who could divine times long past or yet to be. It was whispered that the most powerful among them could re-wryte Time itself. The Source-invokers were also very interesting. They could find Words that could summon up ancient elemental powers within substances and even conjure or create living beings. I recall that Victorie wanted to be one of them. She could have, too. The final sect was the Scrybinders—the one that our Master belonged to. Their job was to edit and repair the works of the other sects so that no Errors would occur. In an existence where the slightest Word could affect the lives of billions, the Scrybinders were most important.

There was also some vague mention of two other sects that no longer existed, but at the time it wasn't that important. But after the mention of the Scrybinders, she told us about how all the Realms were once one great Realm until its Prime Wryter split it into a multitude of Minor Stories when the ancient Scrybes became too ambitious and re-wrote too many of the entity's works. That was the strange thing. The supreme deity in Scrybalism was neither male nor female like Oru, and It never directly interfered with its Creation, unless one radically changed parts of it. It was removed—only a neutral factor in the culture, and not a direct one.

Our Master told us to imagine a Greater Story in which there were many Plots and Subplots within a manuscript that had to be immaculate and flawless. She then told us to imagine what would happen if there were the slightest inconsistency in the Story. That flaw or Error could destroy the whole Story, and so its Wryter had to act to correct that mistake. That was what destroyed many of the ancient Scrybes and segregated the Realms.

I watched her, seeing the awe upon her delicate, ivory face. "Then what is the difference between the Scrybes and the Wryters?"

She laughed at my youthful query. "My dear boy!" she exclaimed. "That question is like asking whether the chicken or the egg came first. There are many answers I could give you. Some among us would have you believe that Wryters are those with only the most limited skill who do not embrace Scrybalism or the Guild. They are just like religious fanatics; an ignorant group who think that all can be converted to their way of thought. Some would rather die…" she sighed, then returned to the topic at hand. "They fail to see that the purpose of the Scrybal Guild is not to be another dogmatic faith like the one you are a slave to, my dear."

It burned then, too. As she spoke those words, I felt the familiar taste of bile rise to my throat as I began to tremble in fury—a fury far too potent to be contained by one so young as I. I felt so limited, so trapped by the false sanctimonies that my religion symbol-ized. Her words cut deep, not necessarily be-cause they were cruel. Some say that the truth can be more painful than the most cleverly crafted of lies. Victorie sensed my mood, and put her hand on my shoulder.

"Do you want to know what my defini-tion is?" my Master asked, more gently, break-ing me away from the rage boiling inside my stomach. "A Wryter is essentially what a Scrybe is—with or without the Guild's train-ing. We do not let the power control us. We master it."

That was one of the many lessons I learned from her; but it was only the beginning.

The years passed, and I kept my secrets well hidden from my family. My father was becoming very popular with the Theocracy hierarchy, and he rose through it. I knew he would eventually be a High Priest. My mother, however, did not fare so well. She died after my siblings grew up. She died in silence. I wish there was more I could have said about her, but my father made sure there was nothing more to be said. According to the tenets of Oru, she was unimportant as a female, and my father would find another Handmaiden to take her place.

One day, as I was heading toward my Master's home in the earliest hours of the morning to continue my lesson, Victorie approached me with a wild, panicked look on her face.

"The Guards!" she panted, her voice hoarse. "They've been after me. They know about us!" As she grabbed my shoulders, I felt a deep, insidious horror worm its way into my gullet. "Your father knows."

We ran into our Master's home, knowing that her Runes of Secrecy would keep us from being found—at least for a while. We hoped to find her and get her aid, but there were times when she wasn't there. Unfortunately, this day was one of them. Then, in the sheer stress and incredulity of the moment, we had another tryst. It was then that Victorie offered me something—something that would haunt me for the rest of my darkest days.

She got off of me and we sat, looking out of a window at the rising sun, the Great Temple's ivory form bathed in a monarch's cloak of crimson gold. Once, I had stared at it and felt religious awe at glimpsing the seat of Oru's servants in the mortal plane. But when I saw it with Victorie, I merely admired it in terms of architecture, no longer in a religious context.

Then again, I lie even now. I don't think I ever had any religious feelings or even reverence for the Light. Perhaps I lied at the beginning of the tale as well. It was more a fear of it that was deeply ingrained into my psyche—a fear of divine retribution. But it existed no longer, as I realized that if that were the case, the Theocracy would have long since been punished for the hypocrisy and corruption they covered up in the name of the Light that they paid lip-service to.

But I knew Victorie's beauty to be genuine—her inner beauty. She sat on the bed, and also stared at the sight. "It might sound strange, but I will miss this place," she turned to look into my eyes. "Let's get out of here. We can leave this place! Together!"

"I don't know." Everything was happening far too fast for my mind to digest. "Let's wait for our Master."

"We can't," Victorie insisted. "We don't have enough time. She will be able to find us, but if we stay there's more of a chance that your father's men will get to us first. Perhaps we can sneak past them now, get to the closest Warp Gate, and find some Realm to take us in."

My mind was reeling. My father knew? For how long? I cursed myself for my carelessness. I had been so busy with my studies and letting my body think for me. I was a fool. Someone must have seen Victorie and I.

"My love," she caressed my cheek, "I'm with child."

I grasped her shoulders and looked her in the eye. "You—you are?"

"Yes," she hugged me. "A baby. You're going to be a father. That is why we have to leave. To make a better life for us—to make a better life for our child."

"I understand. My father will probably be out searching for us. You go to the Warp Gate," and before she could protest, I said, "I will need to get some money if we are to survive. If I get caught, you must go without me. I need to know that you will be safe."

After a moment, she nodded. "Good luck to you."

And we parted ways.

4

When I regained consciousness I found that I was locked in my room, the pure anxiety eating up my entrails as I prayed for Victorie's safety. My trip home had taken an unexpected turn. I remember walking in and hearing my father shout, "You have sheer gall returning here after the abomination you've participated in."

My heart sank as my plan to sneak into my home failed. My father confronted me, two Guards on either side of him. His face was red in livid rage as he struck me across the face, knocking me down. "That's where you've been—with that cheap, heathen whore."

"Don't you dare call her that!" I screamed at him, and I uttered my runes. The invisible force I conjured threw the two Guards by my father's side away. Then I felt something hard and heavy smash down on my skull. I collapsed.

"Black sorcery!" There was horror and indignation in my father's tone. "Warlock-spawn!" I almost didn't recognize my father's voice—either from the pure venom in it or the beginning of unconsciousness. "You dare defy me?" Through my sparkling vision, two more Guards appeared. "Take him to his room. We will find his heathen paramour."

I gathered my books and money, trying to think of some way I could get out of the situation. But then, I saw something materialize through the door—an indistinct black shape.

I stood back and saw it fade away to reveal my Master.

"How did you—?" I started to ask.

"It was a Rune of Cloaking," she interrupted. "I have to get you out of here—now." She grabbed my arm.

"Yes, we have to find Victorie first."

She spared no time in telling me the awful truth. "They have her now." There was pain in my Master's eyes. "I heard that they found her at the Warp Gate. You know what will happen to her. We must go now, to Scryuune. You can have a new life there."

I knew that Victorie was already dead. Heathens were barely tolerated in the City of Light—especially when they interacted with the Sons of Oru. They had to be made an example of. Victorie, her wry smile, and passionate eyes, gone.

"Look!" she shouted through my grief. "We have to go now. She would have wanted you to leave this life behind."

"No," I mumbled, numbness spreading over my chest. "I don't want to go."

"We must. You will die if you stay here! Your first-born status won't save you from execution. Your father knows what you are now!"

"Then let me die!" I snarled, the ache inside of me growing. "Don't you understand? I loved her! And now—"

"No, listen to me," my Master grabbed my chin with what felt like claws of iron. "Listen! She would not want you to." I tried to shake my head. "No! Listen! Victorie wanted what was best for you. She would not want you to stay here, to waste your talent, and die like this. Do you really want to dishonor her memory by being this selfish?"

Finally, I broke away from my Master and paced around the room, letting the barbs of her harsh words take root in the cold soil of my mind. After a moment, I stared at her. "Before I do that, I want you to promise me something."

"What?"

"I want you to teach me," I still felt numb, but my words were clear and concise. "Teach me the Words that I will need to get them—to make them pay for what they did to her! Do you understand?"

"Yes," my Master's dark eyes glittered. "Yes, my Apprentice. Do not worry, I shall."

Under her Cloak of Rune we escaped my house, and the Guards. We eventually came to the Warp Gate—a large monolith with oblong rectangle pillars. My Master whispered something and put her hands on one of the pillars. The space in-between shimmered and convulsed—a pocket of reality becoming fluid enough to allow us passage to another world.

Once, I used to come to this Gate and wonder how they were made, admired the alien beauty of it. Now, I only knew it as an escape-route. A non-wryter could only use the Gate to go to the Realm it was built to transport them to, but an experienced Scrybe could change the trajectory of the energy contained within the structure.

As we left the City of Light, I spared one last look at it. Its beauty was as superficial as its inhabitants, its singular colors and culture intolerant to variation, and my eyes. They killed her. They killed my Victorie. They killed an unborn child. They would pay for this.

Dearly.

5

EVEN I HAD TO admit that the Realm of Scryuune was an experience. There are no actual words that I could use to describe it even now. Thousands of libraries, information centers, and beautiful parks welcomed us. There were people of all skin colors, cultures, religions, and nationalities here. The one thing that they had in common were the wrist-pouches they wore for their own stylized Pens, and the Books they carried under their arms. Knowledge had no discrimination here. Most of the buildings were beautiful as well, inscribed so thoroughly with layers of powerful Runes, that they glowed brightly even at night.

It was quite the shock for me. Then again, the whole experience of getting there was a shock. My Master took me to the Scrybinder district where she had me officially affiliated with the Guild. There was a slight problem when she said I was to have Apprentice-rank and I had to prove my skills to them. In the end, I was accepted although many wondered what sect I would eventually join.

For the most part, I studied under my Master and learned Words of power that would help me gain vengeance on those who had hurt me. It was all I could think about, drowning out even the pleasant sight of this place. Every time I went through a park, I thought of walking beside Victorie, of sharing the things I learned with her; of just being with her. The pain didn't subside—it only worsened. My people back home had poisoned this moment for me. It was another thing I would make them pay for in all due time.

"Come with me," my Master told me one day as we left her chambers. "I am going to show you a secret."

We came to a wall, and my Master whispered her runes. The wall vanished and revealed a dark tunnel. We traveled down the tunnel and through many catacombs before we came to another chamber with a desk, and many dark-covered Books. My Master gestured around us. "This was a secret archive that belonged to a sect long-since dead called the Dark-wryters. It was here that they stored much of their knowledge—knowledge that will help your quest."

I couldn't help but be curious. "Where are they now?"

"Dead, I suppose," she replied. "They were originally made to stop the Chao-scrybes—some uncontrolled, possibly insane wryters. That was why I came for you back in your Realm, to make sure the pain in your head didn't drive you mad and make you into one of them. Let us just say that the Dark-wryters had—questionable methods. The Guild exiled and killed many of them—threatened by their power. I found this place years ago through some old archives. After all, a Scry-binder cannot learn how to fix something if she doesn't know of the damages that are possible. You do promise not to tell anyone of this place?"

"Yes. If you keep your word."

She nodded. "Remember two things from this recent discovery, my Apprentice. Everything has two sides to it—a double meaning. You will learn here things are never what they seem—that even the most literal word can have another meaning entirely."

I drew in her cryptic words. "What are you trying to say?"

"When you go to take your vengeance, do not rush into it blindly," she replied. "Use this knowledge I have given you, and the power that I will give you to plan out what you want. I know you are hurt, but you must not let emotion cloud your judgment. Let emotion be an essence harnessed by form—the form of strategy and careful thought." My Master put a hand on my shoulder. "Assess your situation and your skills, then act. I ask you this because I want you to promise me something."

"What exactly?"

"That you return from this alive. Mistakes of this nature can be fatal. Sometimes vengeance can be one's only motive for living. And when it is gone—what will you do then?"

There was no answer I could give her. I hadn't even given it a thought. What would there be after I did what I had to do?

"You have more potential than you realize. Do not waste it on a meaningless death." Her eyes shone. She caressed my cheek with gentle, spidery fingers. "I already lost one Apprentice, and I do not want to lose another."

"Understood." I was surprised at the intensity behind my Master's voice. "I will do as you say."

"That is all I ask." To this day, I have no real name for the force or emotion that motivated her actions that day.

From that moment on, I studied the forbidden lore there—and prepared.

I did explore Scryuune a bit more. Sometimes I would go for very long walks and reflect on my life, and what I had become. Other times I would do so in order to think of some new ideas for Words. It was one of the former days that I was walking, and I came across a strange sight.

There was an old man in white robes leaning on his wooden staff. He seemed to be waiting for me in the Scrybinder district. I couldn't believe my eyes. This was a Guardian—the highest form of Scrybinder and the equivalent of a Grandmaster. The only times I saw them were when they silently moved about the Scrybinder Archives—guarding them from others to see. I approached the old one.

"There is a great hatred within you, Apprentice," the old man stated, his ancient craggy visage was honest in its years. "A hatred strong enough to not even be placated by Scryuune's Runes of Guardianship. How fascinating, and how sad," he ended. I didn't sense even a hint of jibe in his last comment, however.

The power that surrounded the Guardian impressed me, bathing me in its centuries of wisdom and healing. Despite my afflicted soul, I could respect the years of healing and repair that the old Scrybinder put into everything. But I did not stand down. I looked him in the eyes. "I don't mean you harm. Even if I did, the city's Runes keep me from violence. As you said, I am merely an Apprentice, and you a Guardian. What would you have to fear from me?"

"I am not so sure of that." Whether he meant myself or the effectiveness of the Runes, I will never know. "We fear nothing." There was no defiance or arrogance in his tone, just a calm serenity. "But as a Guardian, it pains me to see a Story such as yours in twain."

That was what Scrybinders did. They repaired the works of other Scrybes—correcting grammar and spelling errors that would otherwise neutralize the effectiveness of their creations, or cause contradictions with horrifying consequences. They also added onto one's wrytings, reinforcing their ideas and words, making them more powerful. But the Guardians took it one step further than their juniors. They saw everything in a much broader, and yet so much more microcosmic sense.

Like the other Guild Grandmasters, they recognized everything as the Greater Story, but they also saw the Minor Stories in the Forms of Realms and people, and how they interacted with each other to make a larger Plot. They also were able to see the flaws in everything, and could even correct potentially disastrous Errors and damage in the Greater Story before they could occur. While the more inexperienced Scrybinders repaired texts, and runes, the Guardians could almost influence Fate itself—the fate of Realms, and of individuals.

It was a pity that it didn't save them from their own destruction.

The old one seemed to be pondering something. Finally, he said, "Come with me, boy."

I was somewhat startled. "Shouldn't my Master know?"

"She will know," answered the Guardian. "Perhaps there is something that you should see."

The old man began to walk back into the Guardian sanctum, his silver-zephyr cloak silently flapping behind his robed body. I stood there, knowing he wanted me to follow him, but I hesitated. The old man turned. "Are you coming, boy?"

It was not every day that one of the Guardians offered to show someone the inside of their domain, never mind a lowly Apprentice. And so, I followed him. He moved fast for an old man, reaching the sanctum gate before I. He raised his staff, and a rune glittered on its grainy surface, igniting a similar rune on the gate. It swung open and we went inside.

It was dark in those halls—the sheer age of them dwarfing even the Guardian that I followed. He nodded wordlessly to many fellow Guardians, and they let us pass toward another door—drifting silently away from us like white-shrouded spectres.

The chamber we entered was vast—and darker than the halls we had passed. It felt as though I was walking on nothing—a sheer pit of nothing. And yet I didn't fall. As we were walking through the majestic gloom, we went past many objects suspended in midair—some of them recognizable like Pens, and Books, but there were strange statues and artifacts that were unfamiliar to me as well.

Finally, we approached a circle of seven Guardians. They formed an ivory ring around what appeared to be a large, red Book with golden threads that seemed faintly serpentine. The Guardians, like the ones outside, didn't say a word as we approached.

"This is a place very few see. We have things here that could be very dangerous. Even the smallest trinket here could destroy a whole Realm." I nodded, weighed by the enormity of his words. "And did your Master teach you about Scrybal lore?"

"You mean the history of the Guild? Yes."

"That is only part of it." The Guardian looked at the hovering Book with its deep crimson cover. "Many a millennia ago, before our Guild existed, the Realms were in primordial anarchy. Wryters did exist in those times, though. But they were different from those you see now.

"They were our ancestors, in some ways, learning how to find the Words that would correspond with the Greater Story. They were also power-mad." His cowl stared away from me. "These individuals were so consumed by their ability, they destroyed themselves and everyone around them. But the most powerful among them, they dared something so terrible it would leave their mark on us forever. They proclaimed themselves gods, and went as far as to act as such."

I recalled something then. "The seventh Scrybal Moral Obligatory Code—Scrybes shall neither deify themselves nor associate themselves with divinity."

"They were the reason we created that seventh rule, and it was with good reason that we did so. These individuals tampered with Creation at such a fundamental level that they lost themselves to the element that they sought. It was when they found what they were looking for that horrors beyond description occurred. Some say that the Great Story itself was made from Chaos. And so we named them Chaoscrybes."

That name was definitely familiar. "They still exist today, don't they?"

"Yes, although they are much scarcer these days, thank the Wryter. They are the reason we put Runes of Stabilization on those we encounter with the latent ability to wryte, like your Master put one on you. The headaches that they experience when their power develops can drive them mad and they scribble words they do not understand—mad scribbles. Long ago, there were those among us who wanted Chaoscrybes killed so that they would be of no threat to anyone. This led to their own downfall and would lead to much more pain among us."

"Why have you brought me here?"

"To see this." He walked up to the Book, touched it, and it opened. The other Guardians raised their rune-inscribed palms against it. And then I felt wonder—wonder and horror all at the same instant. Images beyond description exploded through my mind—terrible things, beautiful things, wondrous manifestations that screamed in a violent joy beyond any human comprehension. They might have been images, but they were without definition—perhaps they had been feelings—or both. Whatever it was, there was fine, crystalline elegance to the explosions that I both visualized and felt.

I felt so alive—and so aware of my own insignificance beside this feat of primal Creation.

Then, just as suddenly, it stopped. The Book's blood-red cover slammed shut on its writhing orange pages. Whatever the Book had summoned up had been locked away from the physical world. But never again would it fade from my mind's eye. The old Guardian looked weary as he glanced at me from the depths of his hood. "That was the creation of a Chaoscrybe whose name and existence are unknown."

"What was it for?" I nearly gasped.

"It might have been a life-tomb." He saw that I didn't understand. "We all have them, in some way. Even you do. Life-tombs contain the personal history of a Scrybe and it also tells of what powerful knowledge he or she has discovered through the years of experimentation. The more potent the Runic vocabulary, the more potent the Scrybe, and the more powerful his life-tomb is. You, my friend, are only beginning yours in that notebook you carry under your arm."

"That might have been his life?"

"Or his mind, or the ideas within it. Perhaps it became one and the same in the end." His eyes glimmered in sorrow. "We keep all such artifacts here under our care so that we can either try to repair them or better understand the forces of Chaos that we fight against. Sometimes, we show them to others..."

"W—why do you show this?" I tried with every inch of my being to make my knees stop shaking.

I knew then that when he spoke, the Guardian's words would forever be immortal to me. "To display both the depths of grandeur and madness that this work is capable of. To serve as a reminder of what wonders can be wrought without any limitations upon raw emotion. And as a warning to those who would pay the price—a price much too high. It is the price of power. There is more we must show you."

Those words haunted me for a long time. But they were nothing compared to the power of that Book. I read other things in the chamber, and found out more about the relationship between the late Dark-wryters and the Chaoscrybes. I knew that what I saw would burn in me.

Forever.

For a long time, I mulled over what the Guardians had made me privy to. I had some serious choices to make, and now, my mind was not as clouded by hatred. What I had seen in their Archives shook me to the very core. Victorie. I was glad she hadn't lived to see what I had seen. I knew that I was dabbling in arts that were banned by the Guild, and that I stood at the proverbial edge of a pit. One step forward, or one step back?

I began to think that perhaps vengeance was not the answer I was looking for. Victorie would never have wanted me to waste my life to avenge her death. The Theocracy—my father—was not worth the effort to destroy. My goal had been a petty one; I was now a different person with a new start. I had a chance to start over, if only we could have together. I still wasn't sure; my soul was in turmoil.

Then one day, I came to my Master's lair. She looked distraught over something. "My

Apprentice," my Master whispered. "There is something I must tell you. Now is the time for your vengeance."

I nodded. I was about to tell her that I was unsure, that I would not act just yet. My Master still kept her back to me.

"There is one other thing," I was silent as I waited for her to say her mind. Something was wrong here. "Victorie..."

"Yes?"

"She is alive."

I froze. "What?"

"When we left your Realm, they didn't kill her. My sources tell me that. They took her, and have held her."

Something inside me twisted. All that time. All that...

"Take me there," I hissed. "Now."

She nodded and pointed to a corridor I had never been down. "There is a Warp Gate there that the oldest sect used for their work. It will take you to where you need to go."

So I plunged into the darkness, not knowing what anything was about anymore, but, by the Word, I would find her. I summoned every shred of hope in my being—hoping that if she had borne a child, it had not been a son.

6

I WENT THROUGH THE secret Warp gate in my Master's underground lair, and looked upon the Holy City once again. It looked the exact same way I left it—when I left her. I looked up and saw the Great Temple in the waning sunset. I knew where I had to go.

After casting a Rune of Cloaking around myself, I walked through the streets, moving toward the cathedral-like structure that had haunted my youth for years. Getting past the Guards, I dispelled my Rune and they moved to attack me.

"In the name of the Almighty Oru, I bless you—" The words of my father were interrupted as I strode past the twisted corpses of the Guards that tried to stop me and entered the sanctuary.

It was bright in there, the diamond mosaics on the ceiling glittering with amber fire. I saw the people stand up and stare at me from their pews in shock and horror. "Blasphemer," I heard someone say, but I ignored it.

My father stood at the altar with a young boy. He looked older, more bent around the shoulders, but the real change was his robes. I knew with his *dedication*, he would make High Priest someday.

He stared at me, and his cold eyes lit up with something like a combination of anger and unease. "You dare to come back here?"

"Where is she?" I bellowed, not noticing the Temple Guards that came forward with their pikes to block my way.

"There is no one here for you!" he shouted back.

"Where is she? Where is Victorie?"

The harshness of my words reverberated through the room. The old man looked at me and gave me a grim smile. "My *wife* is over there."

I saw where he pointed, and the woman rose up from her pew. She was dressed in the conservative, white gown of a clergy member's wife—a Handmaiden. It was much like the dress my mother wore. Her face was heavily lined, and her hair was starting to go white. I stared for a while.

"Victorie?" My mind went numb in horror. She whimpered.

My father's words came back to me from long ago, as cold and imperious as they had always been. "The firstborn son of Oru's divine servants must take the Priesthood that one's father has passed on," my father had stated to me. "But if that son cannot do so, then his own child—a male child—will assume that responsibility."

"No," I murmured. "Victorie—" but as I looked at her, I saw the deadness of her eyes, the lusterless quality of her hair. I knew that after he had broken her, my father had lain with her. I saw the bulge in her abdomen. She was carrying his child.

"When you left, we converted her to our cause," my father said, his pride raking across my soul. "We made her into a proper Handmaiden. It took time, but under my ministrations—"

"Father," said the child, tugging at the hem of my father's golden white robes, "who is this heathen?"

"I am your father," I whispered, moving closer to the child who was my son. But he moved away from me in fear. "Father!" he shouted. "Father! Help me!"

"No, please stop," I begged. I tried to move closer, but the Guards blocked my way with their pikes. "I'm your father. Don't you understand? Victorie! Tell him, please!"

Tears rolled down her eyes, but she said nothing. I realized then that I had been right years ago. Victorie was dead.

"Oru!" the equally dead child who should have been my son beseeched. "Keep this warlock away from me!"

"Be gone from this holy sanctum, vile creature of the Black Arts," my father shouted, but for the first time in my life, I saw fear in his eyes.

"Damn you!" I roared, and I smashed both my hands together, detonating the runes I had drawn on my palms. The Guards in front of me were thrown into the wall, their necks twisted at awkward angles. The congregation screamed and scrambled over each other. I pointed at the main doors to the Temple—the ones I also put runes on. They slammed shut.

I stalked forward, and threw the altar out of my way. My son simply stared at me as I pushed past him toward my father. I knew that I was going to kill him. I didn't know exactly how. I might have ripped him apart with my bare hands, or made his body putrefy on the spot, or beaten him into a bloody pulp. All I knew was that I would kill him for this.

Then I heard my name whispered in a ragged, hoarse voice. I turned around and saw Victorie, her tears streaming down her face. She tried to run toward me, but she tripped over the white dress and fell. I forgot my hatred, and I ran toward her. I held her, and she weakly held me.

"I," she looked up at me with her ravaged face, "I always loved you."

"I know," stroking her hair, my eyes blurred by tears, remembering her vibrancy of youth.

She smiled at me. "You have become so strong, beloved. Please, make the pain go away. Make it go—"

"No," I said, looking at her disheartened face. "No," I repeated, my voice trembling. But then I remembered when we were together, and how gentle she had been, and how open and loving. What passion and fire she had in her. She claimed she would not call any man master. But as I saw the broken expression on her face, I saw the endless beatings, abuse, and pain—watching her child be turned into the thing she hated—I gently traced a shape on her heart.

Her smile was genuine as her eyes rolled up into her head. It was beyond grief. I screamed as I lost her again. Then I saw something in her hand. I moved it and saw the symbol there. I smiled grimly. Now I knew her last wish. I touched the rune. Her body began to change—her arms multiplying, and her legs forming together. She stood up, and began to brown, and her once red hair began to length-en into leaves.

This was what her whole life had amounted to. She must have invested her whole life force into this Altering through the years she had been captive. Her branches smashed through the domed, crystal ceiling and a razor-tipped shower began to fall upon the wailing con-gregates. As I looked up, I saw that her face still existed on the tree she became—a serene, and beautiful visage that rose into the heavens where its beauty had always belonged, away from me.

"Witch!" my father bellowed. "Accursed witch!"

"She will never burn now," I hardly recog-nized the cold, cruel laughter until I realized it was mine. My fingers crackled with flame. "A fitting place." My father backed away from me, his old face slack in horror as I smiled, the feelings I had kept back for so long beginning to resurface in a combination of pleasure and pain. "A fitting place for a funeral pyre—the pyre she will never need. But what has touched her must be purified." I began to sketch my runes in the air.

"No," my father fell to his knees, madness in his eyes. "Please, I beg of—"

He was the first. A stream of flames burst from my hand and struck him. He screamed as the flames enveloped him, charring through his finery, his flesh, muscle, sinew, and bone. Then I looked at the child, the child who looked at me in hatred ... the child who was no longer mine. I killed him quickly. Better that I killed him than to let him become a lifeless, empty drone. Then I unleashed the full power of the rage within myself. I saw the people burn—the people who had stood by, who had blindly followed the Theocracy, who destroyed a work of beauty out of superstitious ignorance. There was also beauty to the crystalline flames I had unleashed—their shade akin to the sunsets I used to watch with her. I turned that beauty into a tool of my vengeance.

The light of many colors exploded everywhere; searing everything in its path. It was so beautiful that it seared my eyes, my heart, and my mind. There was a raw gush of feeling within my chest as something gave, and after a time I wondered whether or not the screams I heard were entirely those of my enemies. I knew after seeing that energy, I would never see anything in quite the same way.

Somehow, I mustered the strength to teleport out of the building before it collapsed into the hollow ruin I had always foreseen it would become.

Even though my eyesight—as I had once known it—had been destroyed by the blast of power I unleashed, I could still *see* what was happening. No longer did I see things in simple opaque colors, or surface texture. It was as though the rainbow fires I wielded had scourged my naked eyes and allowed them to see as the flames did. The carnage I created seemed beautiful as I saw the energy within matter pulse and expand with an almost ephemeral luminescence.

The city was now in eternal sunset—as if some crackling celestial serpents from the waning heavens had come to envelop the bleached white bones of the corpse-like buildings below. That Book of Chaos the Guardians showed me inspired me to do exactly what I had needed. Only the great tree was untouched by my vision of revenge, its roots fertilized by the ashes and blood of its tormentors. I hoped that Oru was ready for the vast number of souls that I had sent him.

"Victory is mine!" I shrilly shouted as they all died in hideous agony. "Do you hear me!

This is my ultimate triumph!" I madly shouted to the Supreme Deity that had never heard my childhood pleas. "On the eve of my Victory!" I broke down and sobbed bitterly, screaming her name over and over again in vain as her visage smiled at me in my mind's eye, forever lost to me.

If my eyes still existed, I don't think I would have even been aware of the City of Light being consumed by the fires of my Words. But now I could visualize it—reduced into ash even as the Great Tree remained untouched. She would forever be untouched. And then it burned. They burned. And so did I. When I looked up, I was barely aware of the change that transformed my eyes, but when I saw the charred pillars devoured by the multi-colored flames I summoned, I began to laugh—a mad, cackling laugh that scared a distant part of myself even as it satisfied the rest of me.

"A tribute," I softly spoke as my laughter died down. "A tribute to my Victorie."

What occurred next was more or less a blur to me even now. Something had happened to my eyes after I drew upon that beautiful flame. Yet in the darkness of my Master's lair, a pale imitation of my old sight asserted itself through my blurred eyes.

"So, you have returned," my Master remarked.

"There are three rites," I remember speaking, feeling hollow and beyond horror.

"Oh? Rites?" she put some puzzlement into her tone.

"Yes; three. The Rite of Sacrifice," the first word painfully squeezed out of my throat. "Succession, and Betrayal. They are for full initiation into the Dark-wryters. But of course, you would know that, wouldn't you?"

"Those are some powerful accusations," my Master stared, not even checking behind her to see me there. "You passed the First Rite."

I fell to my knees as I lost myself in the madness I had so willingly embraced.

She slightly turned from her chair at the desk. "Yes, yes you did. Your eyes have changed, haven't they? It seems that you will wear more than one mark this day," she got out of the chair and stared at me for a long time. Then she opened her arms to me, and I rushed forward, embracing her tightly. After a time, she broke the embrace and asked, "Do you know what a Rune of Unfeeling is?"

I shook my head. "Does it remove emotion?"

"Well, yes and no," my Master looked thoughtful for a moment. "Tell me, my dear one, do you feel pain?" she clinically watched my trembling with an unreadable expression on her face. "I expected as much. It wasn't easy, was it? Destroying all those who tormented you for so long?"

"You—you are a Dark-wryter, aren't you? They were the ones who hunted down Chaoscrybes. Those the Guild exiled when they became corrupt. That was why you let me do this."

"Need I state the obvious?" she sighed. "Yes, but there is so much more to it than that. Haven't I taught you that everything has a double meaning? Yes, we hunted them down. They were Chaos incarnate, power uncontrolled. Look at what their power did to your eyes," she chided. "Too obvious and blatant a power they had. They would have brought too much negative attention down on the Guild. What you do not know is that the Guild unofficially gave us the task of infiltrating the Chaoscrybes and destroying them. But then, one day, the Guild got rid of us when they used us to more or less kill our intended targets."

"You mean when you started taking Chao-scrybal knowledge and *destroying* it."

She smiled. "You amuse me with your dedication to research. The Chaoscrybes were disgusting. They were raw power without any real focus. In fact, the power ruled them. But the Dark-wryters managed to do something no other Scrybe had done—we manipulated the powers of Chaos and translated them into Runic. After all, we had manipulated them, befriended them, and learned their secrets. You see, we tamed this power, gave it focus on a microcosmic level as opposed to the blatantly obvious. We realized that it was more effectively used in subtle ways; in the insidious manner we adopted when we hunted the Chaoscrybes down. And no one questioned our existence——until the Guild developed a conscience. Or maybe when it was revealed to the non-wryter masses that we existed."

"Or perhaps they were afraid of the new horror they created," I hissed, beginning to realize a lot of things about my Master that were starting to make a twisted kind of sense.

"False morality is rather unbecoming of you. They used us and abandoned us. And now we use them—manipulating them behind the scenes. A shadow play, if you will. They like to say Chaoscrybes died out by themselves, and that we were only a bunch of renegades long since killed—although there are rumors that we still have a presence in the Guild. The Guild is like your Theocracy in its dogma and paranoia. It didn't stop you from destroying it and those who worshiped it!"

I didn't say a word. My head was turned away from her piercing, probing, heartless gaze. The shadows of her laboratory hid the tears in my eyes. Then, she smiled and put a gentle hand under my chin. "I know. The Rite of Sacrifice wasn't easy for me the first time either. At least you hated your father," she chuckled, a silvery bell-chiming sound that would have ordinarily been a pleasure to hear. Now it seemed eerie and out of place in those dank surroundings. "I think—Yes, I think I will tell you about the Rune." She went over to her desk and showed me a piece of paper with three partially enmeshed circles crossing over each other.

"That is a heart," I immediately felt foolish for stating the obvious and the raw guilt assailed me anew.

Instead of commenting, she nodded. "Now, watch closely." She held out her wrist with palm upward and removed her Pen from the wrist-pouch. "If you draw a line through this symbol like so," a sideways line was drawn into the left of the heart-construct, "you neutralize most raw emotions so that you can think more logically. This was a common Rune used in the old days—before my sect was officially banished from the Second Circle of Guild Masters—until they realized that another line," she added another sideways line, this time from the right, "would make the heart stop. Remember, only one line in either direction."

She handed me the paper, which I held in trembling fingers, damp from holding them over my eyes. "Does—does all emotion go away?"

"Most of it. Only your triumphs will affect you, my dear one," she cooed. "However, although it will last a long time, and believe me, we Scrybes can live for a very long life, eventually it will pass, and all your feelings will return."

"When?" I was almost gagging from the sheer emotional agony in my heart, doubled over.

"When you are dying, or when death is imminent," there was a strange light in her eyes.

"There is another task for you to complete, Apprentice." Her voice suddenly became cold and formal, walking away from me, she added, "A task in which I think you might need this."

I listened to her mutely as she explained what I had to do. Suddenly, my chest became hollow and void as though I had already used the Rune on myself. "No," I said, "No, I will not use it; not yet."

She turned back to me. "Then you are brave, my dear one," her voice quavered as she briefly brushed her chest with one hand. "Braver than I ever was." She came toward me. I didn't resist.

We made love that night. It seemed to last forever as our bodies enveloped each other with tumultuous feeling and sensation. As she did with me, I traced my fingers down her smooth, white back and stroked some Runes upon it that I learned. She gasped in ecstasy, almost mewling as their power took shape through her flesh. Her spine arched backward as I myself felt the same pleasure explode and reverberate through my manhood.

Once we were finished, we lay in each other's arms for a while. Then, she inserted herself between my legs again into a position where we were more or less sitting. "Do you want to know my name?" she leaned forward, a lock of her silken black hair moved down over her eye, and I brushed it aside. I nodded. Her whisper in my ear was akin to a kiss.

"It is Sakeri."

Sakeri. It was a beautiful name. In Runic, it means Black Widow.

I barely acted in time when she traced her own Runes upon my chest, and my body erupted into pleasurable agony. It was as though all the pleasure she had given to me had transmuted itself into pain. Have you ever noticed that while pleasure is temporary, pain seems to last forever? That was one of the thoughts running through my fevered mind as I willed my hands to stop shaking and trace my own Runes upon her soft breasts.

Through blurred eyes, I saw and felt her writhe in my grasp. With a shaking breath, she continued her pattern upon my flesh with her fingers. As did I continue mine on her. Now that I think of it, it was a combination of pleasure and pain that we both experienced. I dimly knew in the back of my mind that the Runes we were using had the potential to boil the blood of a living creature through intense stimulation of nerve-endings.

It felt so good. It felt as if I were burning up inside. After a while, my sense of discipline began to assert itself. Flesh became Paper, and my fingers became Pens—my body an extension of my will. I sketched out a series of Runes. The combination of ecstasy and agony became secondary as I remembered that flesh could be controlled. It could be manipulated.

It was malleable. The words became a litany in my mind.

Flesh can be controlled...flesh can be manipulated...flesh is malleable...

There was a shriek. And then it was over.

I was panting heavily on top of my Master. She was paler than usual, her thin black hair a tangle, fine beads of dew-like sweat giving her naked body a glimmering sheen. She was breathing shallowly, and I saw blood from the corners of her petal-like lips. But she still lived—for the moment. My Master tried to raise her arms and pull me closer to her. She needed to talk to me. I knew it was no trick.

Her voice was husky with blood. "I—I knew you could do it," her eyes shone brightly. "The ritual is—complete," she coughed, more red staining her lips. "The ritual was different for me, years ago—when I first killed my own Master. But I thought—I thought we could make it special—"

I was wordless, but I stroked her face. She smiled, one that was neither calculating nor shrew. "You know my true name. Now for the Third Rite. I will tell you everything—everything that I can."

There were many things that I found out about Sakeri. What she did to survive her childhood on the streets, what sacrifices she made, and the people that were dead by her own hand and manipulations. Many people. I always wondered how the Priesthood found out where Victorie had been hiding, and where Sakeri had been that day. If she had never died, I might have stayed and never become Sakeri's true Apprentice. She said that Victorie had been too weak a wryter. She needed a strong successor. Like me.

When I looked at her chest, I saw that the Rune of Unfeeling on her chest was dissolving. I knew all that she said to be true. She grasped my hand at the end of her confession, and looked into my eyes. "You know that I love you."

"I know," was my only reply, and with that she contentedly smiled, and closed her eyes.

When it was over, I sketched the Rune over my heart, drawing one line through it.

I had passed the Rite of Sacrifice. I had passed the Rite of Succession. And now I had passed the Rite of Betrayal. I was one of them now—a Dark-wryter—an adept at both creating and understanding double meanings. And I did understand.

My Master had been my mentor, my friend, and my lover. Sakeri was the second person that I loved; a person I trusted more than even myself. She was a person who tried to kill me. She was another victim of my power—the second person I loved who died because of my ambition. From then on I knew that I could not trust anyone—especially not myself. Then, I realized what she had tried to teach me—that absolute power was absolute. Whoever had the most power could use the lust of power in others against them and for one's own singular purposes. Through her death, she finally released me from my illusion of moral-superiority and finished what Victorie had done many years ago. She released me from the guilt, from the fear of my own power.

When I put her Rune of Unfeeling over my heart, I felt nothing.

"My destiny," I recall saying, "Is death…"

Epilogue

AFTER THAT, I DO not recall very much.

Perhaps it was due to the fact that I might have gone mad. Then again, I would still have to feel emotion in order to find insanity, would I not? Do you not just love contradictions? I know that I am a master of them.

I destroyed, I killed, I manipulated, I betrayed, I tortured, and I laughed at it all. I suppose that I did it all for art. Art, you ask? How can I justify my atrocities as art? It is very simple. You see, I realized something about my people—both Scrybes and non-wryters alike.

All people, despite their intentions or appearances, are motivated by darkness. When I say darkness, I mean the basic aspects of human condition—lust, violence, greed, hatred. The list goes on.

The Light that I had been brought up to worship had been an illusion—an illusion fed by false promises and centuries of lies to be large and bloated so that no one would see the truth behind it. But I saw past the immanent bulk that clogged the metaphysical arteries of men. For, behind the Light was an even larger darkness, and in it I saw the truth that I somehow knew all along. Where there is light, there is always shadow. From seeing the Light's secret cloak, I learned the true intentions and ends of humanity.

Don't you understand? Religion is metaphor, and metaphor is expression, and expression is art, and art can be an interpretation of truth—a representation of a fundamental concept in the mortal plane. The reason that my art was unique was that, after a while, it had no need to hide behind masks of sick pretentiousness of *righteousness* and *holiness*. I nurtured a place where one no longer had to play-act the noble or holy man. After all, how can one do such things when one is dead? Everyone is equal in ashes. At least I admit that I am a monster, and I used to wallow in the fact—before it ceased to mean anything to me. I no longer laugh anymore.

And it burns. The Rune that had protected me from myself for thousands of years is now waning, and it burns. All of it, all of what I feel burns in the dark—the dark that has blinded me from long-term exposure. The dark blinded me.

The purpose behind this story was as twofold as the clichéd fork in the road that all people must eventually make choices upon. However, my path—the path of power—was fourfold. As far as I could see, I had many choices in my life. Do not misunderstand; I do not blame what I have done on anyone or anything other than myself.

My testament is my life's story, and my waning is the Last Page. I worked to make the Last Page, only to fail to do the most important thing. When making an end to a story, one must end it. Last Page of my life-tomb, the waning years of my existence, never end. It continues on, poisoning the enthusiasm of the reader, and wryter, until both are hollow inside from disinterest and waste of time. If the ancient Guardians had not been killed as retaliation against the Guild for trying to invade my Great Realm, they would have taken my work and displayed it all for its complexity and creativity—and ultimately show how hollow and empty it really is.

If you are reading this, my successor, then you have destroyed me and taken the power that was mine. Perhaps you too will build a tower that will pierce the very celestial heavens, or create an empire, or a following that will devour whole worlds—and minds. Maybe you will discover new knowledge and enrich your mind with powers in ways I cannot even imagine. Or perhaps you will create something long-lasting in value, like creating your own race to play a god over—a legacy of denizens who will suffer for their origins in your sins that will continue long after your successor comes and ends your burdens.

Rejoice, my destroyer. You have the lore that you have been looking for, and now you can begin to implement your dream of how the world, how the Story, should be. Enjoy the process of building your New Realm, of destroying your foes, and celebrating your achievements. And once again; rejoice. Rejoice for the end that is your right. Pray for the end to come to your Story so that it too can be added to the shelves of volumes behind this throne of those who came before you. Or build another shelf for all I care. It matters not to me now.

But if your end does not come, or if you destroy it—then cry, my friend. Cry for the sacrifices you made, the friends you lost, the family you abandoned, the lovers you betrayed. All in vain, my friend—all in vain. Have you ever written yourself into a corner? Let me explain what it is like. It is a personal, perpetual, dark hell of your own making—the wasteful redundancy that you will find both yourself and your creations wallowing in if you do not end the latter before your inspiration burns itself out. Cry if you destroy the one who will be your undoing before he or she is done. That was why the one before me let me live—to serve as the instrument of her demise. And that was why I, too, had the foresight of mind to let you live. Cry, if your Story becomes trite and numbing to reader and wryter like fast-acting poison.

Cry, when you feel the waste of all that potential you once had. Cry when you no longer love the things you make. Cry when you become the living waste that you have begun to embody.

And so, I leave you now. Another Grandmaster of the Dark-wryter sect passes, my Story ended——and your hell has only begun.

May your Last Page end well.

Also by Richard Fierce

WEBSITE

www.richardfierce.com

FACEBOOK

www.facebook.com/dragonfirepress

FANTASY

Dragon Riders of Osnen Prequels

The Price of Honor

Wings of the Fallen

Dragon Riders of Osnen

Trial by Sorcery

Bound by Blood

Chosen

Acolyte

Sworn

The Fallen King Chronicles

Dragonsphere

The Fallen King

The Valiant King

The Restored King

Magic and Monsters

The Wizard and the Frog

Spellbreather Novels

Smoke and Blood

Anthologies

Chronicles of Mirstone

Magic of Mirstone

Quests of Mirstone

Dragon Riders of Mirstone

Standalone

Shard of the Sun

SPACE OPERA